I AM READING
Princess Rosa's Winter

JUDY HINDLEY

ILLUSTRATED BY
MARGARET CHAMBERLAIN

KINGFISHER
BOSTON

KINGFISHER

a Houghton Mifflin Company imprint
222 Berkeley Street
Boston, Massachusetts 02116
www.houghtonmifflinbooks.com

First published by Kingfisher in 1997
This edition published in 2005
2 4 6 8 10 9 7 5 3 1
1TR/0904/AJT/FR(SACH)/115MA/F

LIBRARY OF CONGRESS CATALOGING–IN–PUBLICATION DATA
has been applied for.

ISBN 0-7534-5859-4
ISBN 978-07534-5859-4

Printed in India

Contents

Chapter One

It was a winter morning
long ago.
Inside the castle
it was dark and cold.
When Princess Rosa first woke up,
the candle by her bed
was still lit.

Princess Rosa asked her nurse,

"Why is it so dark

when we wake up?"

Nurse Bonny said to her,

"Because it's winter.

The sun does not rise

until very late now.

Winter is a dark time."

Nurse Bonny blew on the fire

to make it blaze.

But when the small princess
jumped out of bed,
she still felt cold.
She put on
one gown
over
another—
but she still felt cold!
She said,
"It is too cold today!
Why is it so cold?"
Nurse Bonny said,
"Because it's winter.
The sun is tired,
and the snow is falling.
A dark world is a cold world."

6

Rosa huddled with her dogs
beside the fire.
Nurse Bonny
toasted bread
and warmed some cider.
Every morning
breakfast was the same—
but they ate every scrap.

Then they put on their
cloaks and hurried off
to say good morning
to the King and Queen.
Icy breezes whistled
down the hallway.
Cold, white mist
crawled along the
floor.

It was so cold that
the King and Queen
were still in bed.
"Climb up here,
my little climbing rose!"
the King called out.
"Come and kiss me,
my sweet Rosa!"
cried the Queen.
So she did.
The royal bed had a
canopy and curtains.
Inside it was like a big,
warm cave.
It was very cozy.

But here came

the King's head servant

to tell the King

about important business.

And here came

the Lord High Chancellor

to ask the King

a very important question.

And here came the priest

to say a prayer

with the Queen.

And here came her maid

to do her hair.

And here came the cook
with a big tray of breakfast
and a little page boy
with a message.

The doors were guarded
by the royal watchmen.
But the cat sneaked past,
and the royal dogs barked,
and finally, the King said,
"Enough!
Everyone must go!"
So they did.

Chapter Two

Off went the princess,

her nurse, and her dogs.

Along the misty hallway,

down a twisty staircase.

Out they went
through the huge doors
of the castle.
But outside
big, wet flakes of snow
were falling.

It was too cold
to take the dogs out
for a walk.

It was too cold
to take the pony
for a ride.

It was so cold that
the falcon
wouldn't fly.

They couldn't even feed
the ducks and fish.
The fish were hidden
underneath the ice.
The ducks and geese and
swans had flown away.
The small princess was cold.

Back they went
through the huge doors
of the castle.
It was dinnertime.
Everyone gathered
in the great hall,
and a big fire blazed.
But everyone was gloomy.

For weeks and weeks

they had not heard

any news

or one new song

or one new joke.

Everyone was bored.

When dinner came,

they were gloomier than ever.

"Same old thing again!"

said Princess Rosa.

"Can't I have an egg?"

"Oh, my darling,

there are no eggs in the

winter," said the Queen.

"When the days are dark,

the hens don't lay them."

The small princess

threw down her spoon.

She cried,

"I don't like the winter!"

"Hush!" said Nurse Bonny.

"Winter has some good things."

"Name one,"

said Princess Rosa.

Everyone thought hard.

"I'm sure there are

some good things,"

said the old knight.

"I know!"

cried the little page boy.

"Snow!

It is good for sleds

and good for sliding,

and it is great for snowballs."

But the King said,

"There is one good thing

that nobody has mentioned.

Hode."

"Who is Hode?"

asked Princess Rosa.

But just then,

CRASH!

The castle doors flew open.

WHOOOO!

The winter wind

came whirling in.

Chapter Three

There in the doorway

stood a huge, white, furry creature.

Everyone was quiet.

The furry creature

marched up

through the hall,

dripping snow.

The wind roared.

The fire crackled.

The drips of melted snow

said, "Hiss!"

The creature kneeled
before the King and Queen,
bowing low.

Then it stood up.

It shook off the snow.

It threw off its bearskin.

"It's Hode!" cried the King.

"It's our wonderful winter visitor."

"It's Hode!" cried the Queen

and the knights

and the watchmen.

"It's Hode!" cried the ladies

and the servants

and the fiddlers.

"Hooray!" cried everyone.

"Hooray!"

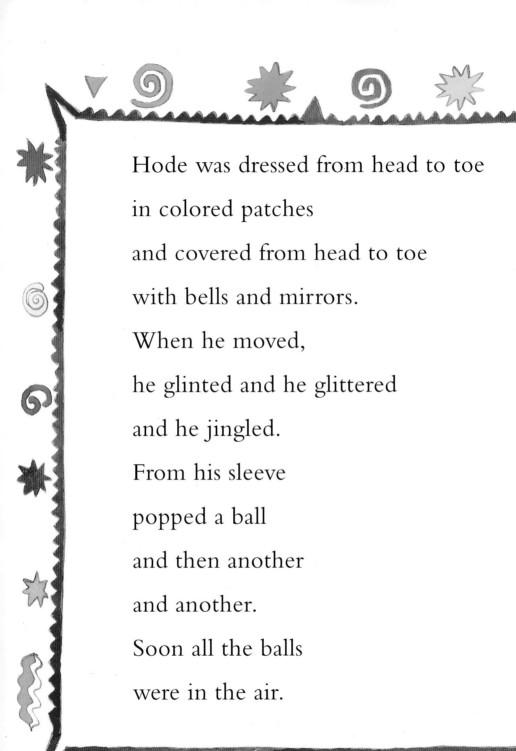

Hode was dressed from head to toe

in colored patches

and covered from head to toe

with bells and mirrors.

When he moved,

he glinted and he glittered

and he jingled.

From his sleeve

popped a ball

and then another

and another.

Soon all the balls

were in the air.

He juggled them high,

he juggled them low,

he juggled them around his arms

and legs

and body.

He whistled them
into his hat
and out his sleeve
and back!

And then he did 11 somersaults
and 13 backflips.
When he finished,
everyone clapped
and shouted.

"Hooray!" cried everyone.
"Hooray!"

The king was so excited
that he could not stop
giving orders.
He cried,
"Bring me a bowl of apples!
Bring some walnuts!
Bring some chestnuts!
Bring the fiddles!
Bring some good red wine
for us to drink!
It's time to celebrate!"
"Of course," said the Queen,
"Why wait for Christmas?"

Soon

everyone was dancing,

and throughout the long, dark
winter night they danced and played.

Very late that night,

when the little princess

had gone to bed,

the snow had stopped.

Her nurse opened the shutter

just a crack,

and they peeked out.

The moon was huge and white.

The bright snow gleamed

almost as bright as daylight.

"The snow is beautiful,"

said Princess Rosa.

"And Hode is wonderful,"
she said.

"And dancing is fun!"
she added.

"Ah," said the little princess,
"I can't wait until Christmas!"

About the author and illustrator

Judy Hindley lives near an ancient forest in a town built in the time of knights and castles. Judy says, "I like winter because it's one of the best and coziest times for reading books."

Margaret Chamberlain is interested in how people lived long ago. She says, "Life must have been hard. The seasons really ruled people's lives. But, as Princess Rosa finds out, they also had a lot of fun!"

Strategies for Independent Readers

Predict
Think about the cover, illustrations, and the title
of the book. What do you think this book will be about?
While you are reading think about what may
happen next and why.

Monitor
As you read ask yourself if what you're
reading makes sense. If it doesn't, reread, look
at the illustrations, or read ahead.

Question
Ask yourself questions about important ideas
in the story such as what the characters might
do or what you might learn.

Phonics
If there is a word that you do not know, look carefully
at the letters, sounds, and word parts that you do know.
Blend the sounds to read the word. Ask yourself if this is
a word you know. Does it make sense in the sentence?

Summarize
Think about the characters, the setting where the
story takes place, and the problem the characters faced
in the story. Tell the important ideas in the beginning,
middle, and end of the story.

Evaluate
Ask yourself questions like: Did you like the story?
Why or why not? How did the author make the story
come alive? How did the author make the story fun to
read? How well did you understand the story? Maybe
you can understand it better if you read it again!